Fiddler T. Bear

Written by

Stephen Cosgrove

Illustrated by

Wendy Edelson

HERITAGE BUILDERS

Stephen stuff: http://www.stephencosgrove.com

For ancillary rights information: stephen@bookpop.com
For publishing rights: info@heritagebuilders.com

HERITAGE BUILDERS   3105 Locan Avenue, Clovis, California 93619

Dedicated to Eugene (Gene) Russell. Neither bear nor bunny, but rather a dear friend for well-over lebinty-billion years.

Stephen Cosgrove

arther than far and to the very edge of the horizon is a path bordered in lacy fern. Follow that path as it twists and turns this way and that. Go this way, go that way, and soon you will find yourself in the land of Barely There.

Watch as the wind whips a leaf high
into the sky and then disappears before
you can blink your eye.

Barely There, a land filled with
wondrous delight.

Barely There, where the forest,
wrapped in evergreen velvet, softly echoes
with the words…

… Barely There

… Barely There.

As you walk this path on your way to somewhere, anywhere in the heartland of Barely There, you will pass a cool, shadowy glade, a meadow if you would. Here, nestled just off the path are three rustic cabins made of pitchy-pine and poplar, and it is in these three cabins that there live three very reclusive bears, the Hideaways.

No matter the time of day or night, their shutters are always closed, giving the impression that no one is ever home.

But don't walk on thinking you have seen all that you could have seen here. If you look carefully, you will see thin wisps of smoke spiraling from the twisted, rusted chimneys like thieves slipping into the night. Look there and there, and there; doors creak open, shutters unbar, as blinking eyes peer out at you.

These are the Hideaway bears, but don't expect them to greet you. For the Hideaways don't trust anyone, and if the truth be known, they barely trust each other.

The Hideaways would have stayed hidden away, maybe forever, wrapped in their own suspicions, had not, one day, there come whistling down the path, a stranger bear as bold as could be.

This bear didn't sneak from tree to tree like the Hideaways. This bear didn't hide at all. He danced down the path, light on his feet, whistling a merry tune. Nonchalantly tucked beneath his arm was a mysterious, odd-shaped package not wrapped in paper, but rather in the soft folds of well-woven cloth.

He nearly walked right on by the cabins, so hidden were they, but then the smoke sneaking into the skies from the chimneys caught his eye. He smiled a secret smile, stepped off the path, walked right up to the first of the cabins and knocked on the door not once, not twice, but thrice.

Rap! Rap! Rap!

From inside the cabin he could hear the flopping sound of fuzzy slippers slapping on worn wooden floors. With a squeak and a creak the door opened and there stood one of the Hideaway bears dressed in a woolen dress and a dusting cap perched upon her head.

Nervously she blinked her eyes and looked about. "Who are you and what do you want?" she growled.

That bear just grinned a big old grin and said. "My name is Fiddler, and you see I come from the land of Frippery. I have traveled far and am really beat. May I come in and rest my feet?"

Then, without an "Excuse me!" or even a "By your leave!" he bustled right into the cabin.

Not knowing exactly what else to do, she followed him inside and closed the door.

Fiddler plopped himself down in a big overstuffed chair set beside a table, worn smooth by years of clay potter's plates being slid across. He set his package gently on the table, smiled warmly, and asked, "I've told you my name, I would never mislead, now who might you be, yes, indeed?"

"Well, uh, my name is Opal L. Bear," she said just as nervous as could be.

Fiddler chuckled, "Then that's what I will call you, I do declare. And so, do you have some food you'd be willing to share?"

Opal squinted her eyes and said, "Well, Mister Fiddler Bear, folks in these parts brag far and wide about my barley bran biscuits. They are very, very good. But I am not in a mind to share without knowing first what you'll be giving me in return!"

Fiddler drummed his fingers on the table and laughed, "Your biscuits are great, this I've been told, and for them I'll trade you something with more value than gold!"

"Hmm," she thought, "more value than gold?" Then, without a second thought, she laughed, "Alrighty then, you shall have your biscuits, Mr. Fiddler Bear."

From two sacks she poured bran and barley into
a bowl. She added two eggs, a cup of milk, three big
spoonfuls of sugar and a pinch of salt. She whisked
and whipped all into a batter that was better than any
other. Once mixed, she plopped the batter into biscuit
tins and slid them into the oven. As the biscuits baked,
she danced about the cabin, her skirts skittering on
the floor as Fiddler clapped his hands and hummed a
ragtime tune.

When the biscuits were done, Fiddler ate every
single one. Then, he patted his belly and said, "Those
biscuits were fine, tasted just great, but something was
missing in what I just ate!"

Opal began pacing about muttering, "I know, I know, I know! Bumble-berries are what is missing! That miserly old *Alva V.* Bear who lives right next door won't give me any bumble-berries from his prickly patch to make my biscuits better. If I asked *Alva V.* for berries, he'd just ask for biscuits in return."

"*My, oh my,*" laughed Fiddler with a smile. "Think I'll just slip next door and talk with *Alva* for awhile." He picked up his package and was out the door quicker than you could say, better baked barley bran biscuits three times.

With Opal Bear peeking through her shutters, Fiddler brazenly swaggered next door. With his hat in his hand he knocked loudly, not twice, not thrice, but four times: Rap! Rap! Rap! Rap!

There was a bumping and a rustling inside, and then the door opened wide and out stumbled old Alva V. Bear, dressed in his red winter underwear.

"Who are you and what do you want?" he grumbled.

"My name is Fiddler, and you, you see, I come from the land of Frippery. Hungry I am. Hungry I'm very. May I share your bumble-berries?"

"Well I don't just share. These are special berries from my personal prickly patch."

Fiddler just smiled and then whispered, "Your berries are great, this I've been told, and for them I will trade you something with more value than gold!"

"More value than gold?" muttered Alva V. "Hmm, I like the sound of that. Yes, sirree, Mr. Fiddler Bear, you shall have some of my berries, yes indeed!"

With that, the two quickly slipped inside and closed the door.

Fiddler plopped himself down on a rocking chair. He sat there smiling as he rocked back and forth, back and forth. He didn't say a word.

Alva V. Bear was as nervous as could be. No one, not a single soul had ever sat at his table before, let alone waiting to taste his berries. But what Fiddler had was better than gold, so berries it would be. Alva V. grabbed a burl bowl of highly polished pine from the shelf and filled it to the brim with bumble-berries all purple and plump and set the bowl down with a thump.

Fiddler tasted one, then two, then twenty, and soon all the berries were gone. He leaned back in the chair, wiped his mouth with the back of his hand and said, "Those berries were fine, they tasted just great! But something was missing in what I just ate."

"I know! I know! I know!" said an agitated Alva V. Bear. "Honey from the butterbees is just what was missing! But the butterbees and their honey belong to Barbara B. Bear. If I asked for honey, she'd just want bumble-berries in return!"

"Well, well," said Fiddler with a smile, "think I'll go talk with Barbara for awhile!"

Fiddler grabbed the odd-shaped package, slipped it beneath his arm and fairly skipped down the path and up two wobbly steps that led to the porch of the cabin of Barbara B. Bear. He rapped firmly upon the door.

There was a long pause, but finally the door slowly opened. There, standing in the threshold, was Barbara B. herself. "Who are you and what do you want," she asked shyly.

"Well," began Fiddler with a smile, "My name is Fiddler, and, you see, I come from the land of Frippery. Hungry I am, but I have no money. Still and all, could I taste your honey?"

"No money, huh?" she grumbled and growled. "Then why should I give you a taste of my honey?"

If it were possible, Fiddler's smile grew even broader. "Your honey is great, this I've been told, and for a taste I'll trade you something with value greater than gold."

"Value greater than gold, you say?" she asked, crooking her finger, inviting him in. "Please come inside Mr. Fiddler Bear. A taste of my honey you shall have, indeed."

Sitting in the center of the cabin was a large, metal-staved wooden cask. Hanging from a pine peg on the wall nearby was a wooden spoon. Barbara B. grabbed the spoon and dipped it into the cask, twisting and twirling it round and round. Finally, she lifted the spoon, now all coated with honey, golden as the sun and nearly as thick as warm salt-water taffy.

She handed the spoon to Fiddler, who slowly licked it clean, right down to the grain of the wood. "My, oh, my!" he smiled. "That honey was fine, it tasted just great! But there was something missing in what I just ate!"

Barbara B's smile twisted into a scowl faster than you could say better beware, butterbees barely buzz boldly. "I know! I know! I know!" she said.

"Biscuits and berries would taste great with my honey, but those Hideaway bears won't give me any. If I asked, and I won't, they'd just want some of my honey in return."

Fiddler stood there for a moment with the odd-shaped package tucked under his arm, and then, without a 'how do you do!' he walked out on the porch and closed her door.

As the sun slowly set, Fiddler stood in the clearing near the Lacy Fern Path and then carefully placed the odd-shaped package on a broad-based stump. With three sets of eyes peering through the shutters of three different cabins, Fiddler began collecting bits of sticks from the forest floor.

He carefully stacked the wood in a pile near the odd-shaped package and with the strike of a wooden match he set it ablaze.

For the first time in a long time, the forest glade glowed as the flames licked around the dry sticks and branches. Smoke swirled and curled through the boughs and branches of the trees like a ribbon wrapped around a present.

The fire crackling and snapping, Fiddler picked up the package and sat down on the old wooden stump and carefully began to unfold the wrapping.

There, nestled in the cloth, was a highly-polished fiddle, hand-carved out of rare bonewood, with a matching bow. The strings, strung tightly across the neck, glistened in the firelight like the silken strands of a spider web drenched in morning dew.

His great paws caressed the fiddle and he dreamily placed it under his chin and began

passing the bow across those delicate strings.
Music began to pour like water bubbling down a
dry creek bed. Music, mysterious, wonderful music
washed over the dark and shadowy glen.

And then, a miracle of sorts occurred as one
by one the doors of the cabins opened, one, two,
three. There, standing openly on their porches
were Opal L, Alva V, and Barbara B.

The three Hideaway bears listened for a time, and then each in turn went back inside their cabins and rustled about.

In a moment or two, they stepped off their porches and in single file moved toward the fire and the music. In their hands they carried those things they had greedily hoarded all these years: barley bran biscuits; purple bumble-berries; and a crock of butterbee honey.

They stood there, gently swaying to the music

and when Fiddler finally stopped playing, they quickly gave him their treasures in exchange for the music he had just played.

Fiddler smiled and said, "I was paid before, and now my payment is owed, and as I said before it is more valuable than gold. But it's not the music, the music I give, the payment is 'sharing' -- the only way to live. Now share with each other your biscuits, berries, and honey; for you'll find sharing friendship is better than gold or money."

Then he tuned his fiddle,
rosined his bow, and with a tap of
his foot, he let it all go.

And from that day forward
the Hideaway bears, not hidden
anymore, shared everything, as we
all do…

…in the land of Barely There.

Serendipity Books
collect them all

Sniffles | Number 1   Buttermilk | Number 2   Creole` | Number 3   Fanny | Number 4

Flutterby | Number 5   Leo the Lop | Number 6   Morgan & Me | Number 7   MuffinDragon | Number 8

  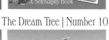  

Bangalee | Number 9   The Dream Tree | Number 10   Ming Ling | Number 11   Sassafras | Number 12

Kartusch | Number 13   Squeakers | Number 14   Trafalgar True | Number 15   Zippity Zoom | Number 16

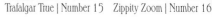

www.heritagebuilders.com

And from that
day forward the Hideaway
bears, not hidden anymore,
shared everything, as we
all do
    ...in the land of
Barely There.

Serendipity
Visit us at - www.bookpop.com

HERITAGE BUILDERS
www.heritagebuilders.com

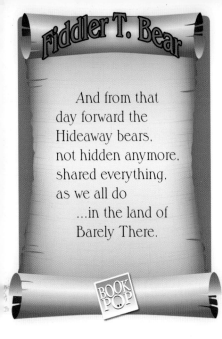

Fiddler T. Bear

And from that
day forward the
Hideaway bears,
not hidden anymore,
shared everything,
as we all do
...in the land of
Barely There.

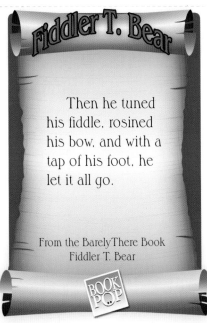

Fiddler T. Bear

Then he tuned
his fiddle, rosined
his bow, and with a
tap of his foot, he
let it all go.

From the BarelyThere Book
Fiddler T. Bear